moO

For Matt—who shifted my perspective and helped me discover a deeper compassion for others. This one's for you. Let's change the script.

MASCOT KIDS!
an imprint of Amplify Publishing Group

www.mascotbooks.com

Can I Tell You About My Brother?

For more information, please contact:
Mascot Kids, an imprint of Amplify Publishing Group
620 Herndon Parkway, Suite 320
Herndon, VA 20170
info@mascotbooks.com

Library of Congress Control Number: 2022908534

CPSIA Code: PRT0922A

ISBN-13: 978-1-63755-024-3

Printed in the United States

CAN I Tell You ABOUT MY Brother?

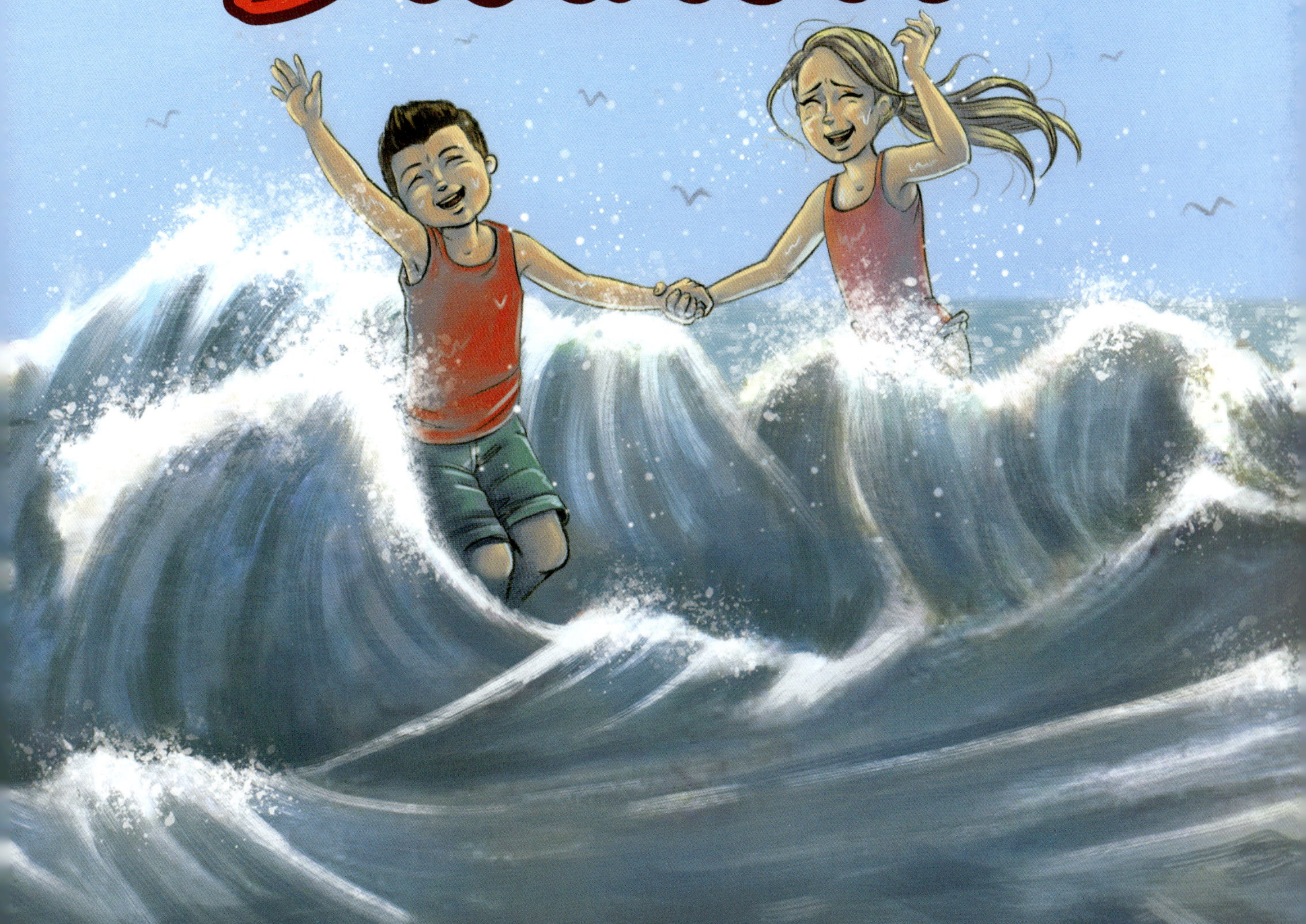

Rebecca H. Vaughn

Illustrated by Chiara Savarese

Can I tell you about Brady?
He's my little brother.
We like to laugh when he pulls out his secret stash of costumes,
and we get creative and *Really Silly.*

Brady has a fun imagination. He asks me questions like:

"Would you rather cuddle with three dinosaurs . . .

. . . or chase after a very bad guy?"

"Hee

Hee

Hee!"

Brady is different from my other brothers though.
Momma says he is autistic.

What is **Autism?** I wonder.

Others might wonder . . .
Why is he nervous to share his things?
Why do his eyes look scared when he is in crowded stores?
Why does he put stuff in his mouth?
Why does he want to talk about the same thing over and over?
Why does he ask the same questions again and again?

I wonder about these things too.

Sometimes Brady
makes **LOUD** sounds
over and over. I try to make him stop.
But sometimes I can't, and I have to leave the room.

I don't know why he makes loud sounds.
Momma says it is comforting to him.
I like to comfort myself with my soft pink blanket. Do you know the color pink makes me happy?

Brady isn't always loud, though. We like to sneak upstairs and talk in his bedroom.
His brain thinks about numbers.
He can add big numbers without writing them down.

My brain thinks about stories.
He enjoys when I read the animal and princess adventures I create in my pink notebook.

When my brother is excited, he holds me tightly and presses his head into my body.

Momma says the pressure is calming to him.
He's learning to ask for a hug when he needs one, and when he asks, I squeeze him with all my might.

"Brady,
do
you
need
a
Hug?"

It can be too tight of a hug for some, but not for me, and certainly not for Brady.

Momma says everyone has special abilities, and some people have the same talents. Well, guess what? Brady and I are both artists! My brother presses hard into paper with his broken crayons to create giant rainbows.

We both like to use a lot of color, but I'm a different kind of artist than Brady.

His art makes me smile. One time he drew a huge bird and small puffy trees.

"Look at my picture. Do you see what it is?"

He also likes making pictures of himself.

Brady's autism also means that he asks questions over and over.

"What does *holy moly* mean?"

"When should I say *holy moly*?"

"What do bad germs look like?"

"Do hugs make my heart grow three times bigger?"

"Does winter not like spring?"

It's tough to answer Brady. His questions can be hard. When I try to answer, he seems like he isn't listening. This bothers me.

I can get frustrated because I don't always want to answer his questions. Momma says his brain can get stuck on a topic, and we try to help him get unstuck.

So I answer him once, then ask him another question. Sometimes, I just say, *"Come on, let's go play!"*

My brother's autism also means that he **STOMPS** around our house, even jumping down the stairs.

Momma says he likes the way the heavy stomping feels on his feet.

I don't like the loud stomping.
I tell him to go outside if he wants to be a dinosaur.

When we are outside, my brother climbs and hangs upside down. This makes him so happy.
I like to practice my cartwheels. It's how I like to flip myself upside down.

At my local beach, people call him the crab digger. He digs the deepest holes and pulls out live, cranky crabs!

We put them in my big purple bucket. I tell him when we need to let them go.

To get the sand off, we run into the ocean together to jump the waves. Brady gives the waves names depending on their size.

Bob is always the biggest.

We laugh as the waves knock us down again and again. Momma says the pressure of the waves makes Brady happy.

Sometimes my brother talks to other people we see on the beach. I've seen him walk around showing beach-goers beautiful shells he has found near the shore.

Momma says Brady enjoys talking to people who show an interest in what he likes. He's brave while I often feel shy. I'm trying to be braver like Brady.

CLAP
CLAP

My brother doesn't always enjoy people. Brady gets really uncomfortable in some places. His eyes fill with tears when we go to a crowded store. He doesn't like a lot of people in a small space. I don't think he likes the noise either.

Momma says he has anxiety. That means he feels scared and can't help it. So I grab his hand and find more space. Sometimes Dad has to take him outside while Momma finishes her shopping.

I think he just needs a *Break.* A break from *Everything.* A quiet place.

I like breaks too. When I get home from school, I spend time alone in my room playing with my sparkly pink slime.

I may not know exactly what autism is, but I do know that my brother has feelings, cares about others and how they treat him, and likes to do some of the same things I find fun.
By hanging out with Brady, I know that he has amazing art abilities, an eye for beachcombing, and fearless climbing skills.

My brother is different, just like you are different and unique. Momma says this makes us all special and worthy to be known.

Why fit in when you were born to stand out?
Dr. Seuss
SHELLS

The more time I spend with my brother, the more I get to know him.

I think that if other kids spent time with my brother, they would like him too. He's my friend, and he makes me laugh. Do you have friends who are different than you?

If you see a kid who seems a bit like my brother, remember that he wants to be seen. So smile and say "hi."

Don't be surprised if he shows you his latest creation or asks if you'd rather climb the highest mountain or jump out of an airplane with a dinosaur.

He's just like you, only a little different. And what makes him unique is what I admire the most.

COLOURS
CRAYONS

Rebecca Vaughn writes about her son, Brady, and her daughter, Alexis, in her heartfelt book about autism and sibling relationships. When she isn't daydreaming about other book ideas, she is walking, talking to herself, biking, or painting while cramming in multiple grocery store runs to keep up with her four young kids. In her spare time, she teaches high school mathematics and reflects on the powerful impact that compassion and empathy have in cultivating acceptance of all individuals.

You can keep up with Brady, Alexis, and family at BeingBrady.com.

moo

moo

moo

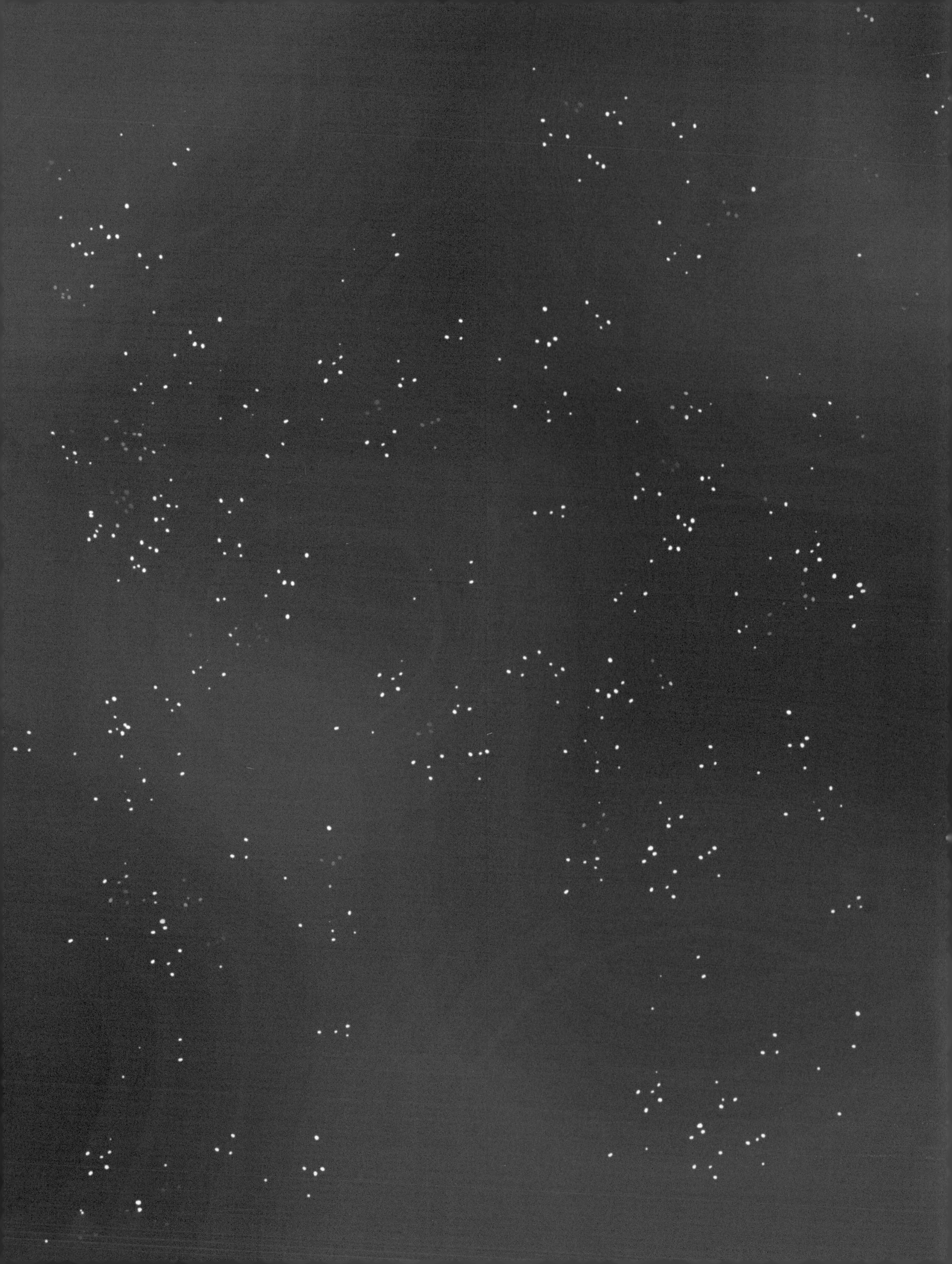

Dedicated to all children around the world
Spain
India
Russia
Mexico
Thailand
USA
Scotland
Holland
China
Saudi Arabia
Ghana
Japan

MASCOT KIDS!

www.mascotbooks.com

Mr. Toad's Adventures: My First Dental Examination

For more information, please contact:
Mascot Books
620 Herndon Parkway, Suite 320
Herndon, VA 20170
info@mascotbooks.com

Library of Congress Control Number: 2021917806

CPSIA Code: PRT0122A
ISBN-13: 978-1-64543-458-0

Printed in United States

MR. TOAD'S ADVENTURES

My First Dental Examination

Tim Carpenter

Illustrated by Rachel Novel

"Professor Toad, what should I expect during my first dental appointment tomorrow?" asked Little Tadpole.

With a kind smile and a wave of his hand, Professor Toad asked Little Tadpole to have a seat.

Always
Brush
and
Floss!

"Well Little Tadpole, you will go through some new things and in many different rooms," Professor Toad began.

"After you have signed in with the receptionist or nurse, your mommy or daddy will be asked to fill out some necessary paperwork. When your paperwork has been completed, you can take them back to the nice lady at the front desk. The nurse will start a patient chart for you that will hold all your information from the checkup and X-rays taken throughout your visit."

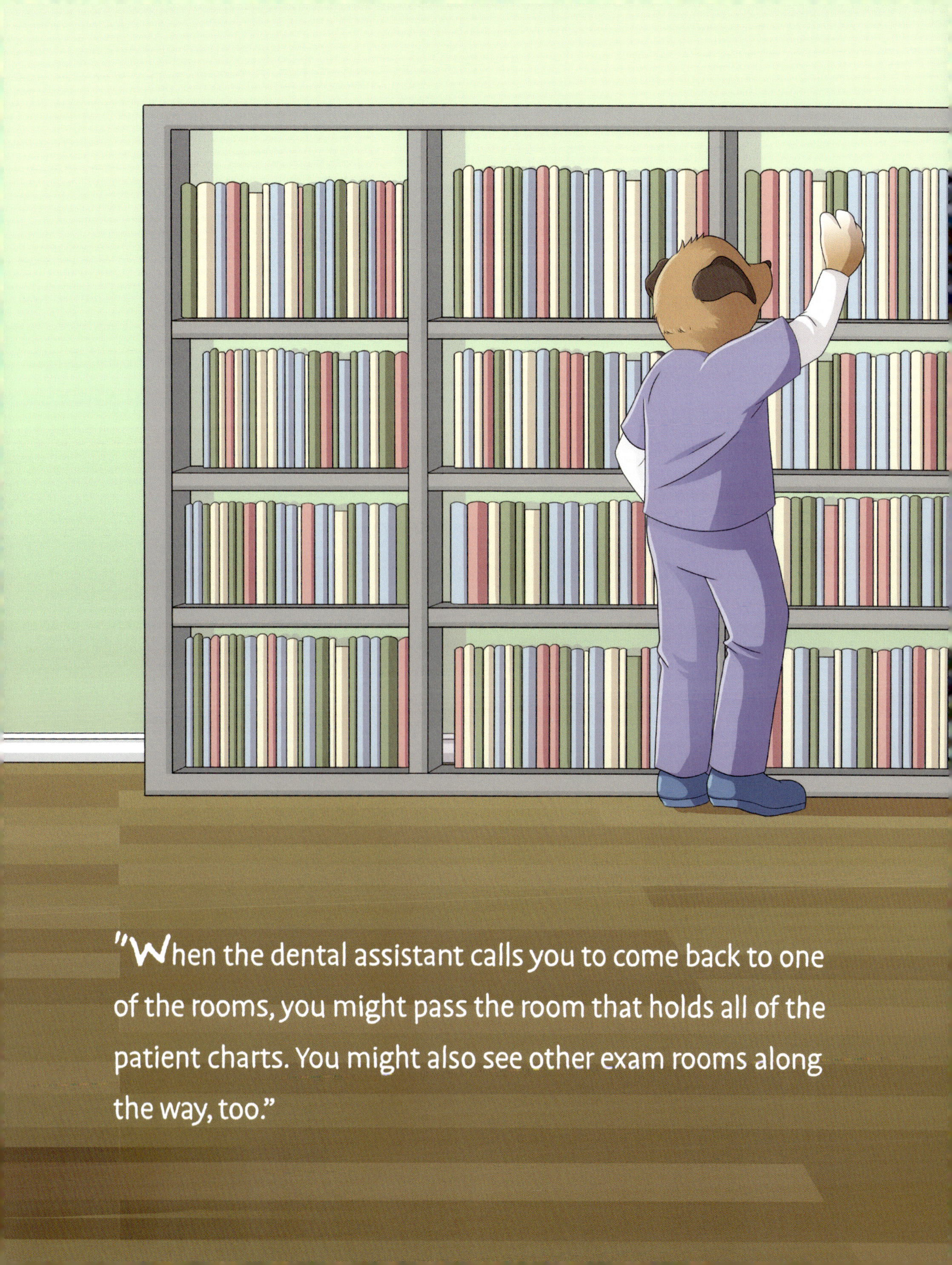

"When the dental assistant calls you to come back to one of the rooms, you might pass the room that holds all of the patient charts. You might also see other exam rooms along the way, too."

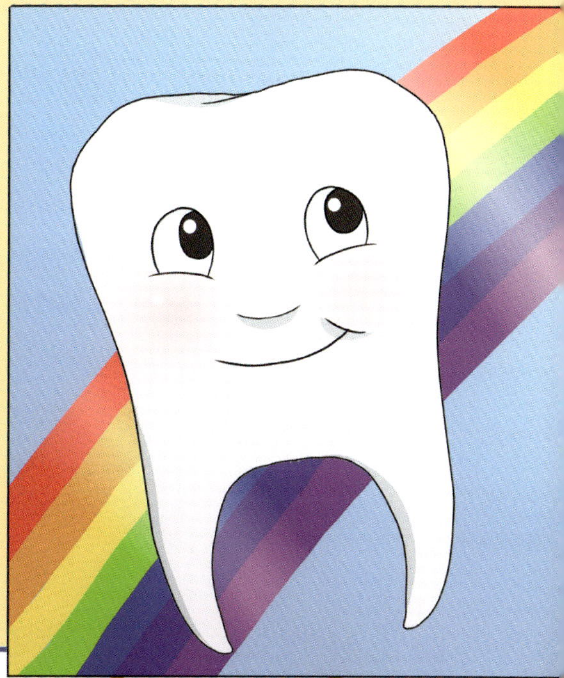

"The dental assistant will have you climb up into the patient chair and demonstrate how the chair is maneuvered: up, down, and backwards. The dental assistant will explain the equipment that will be used by the doctor. Once you are settled and comfortable in the chair, the dental assistant will review your chart, and verify your medications, medical history, and any health issues," Professor Toad said, warmly.

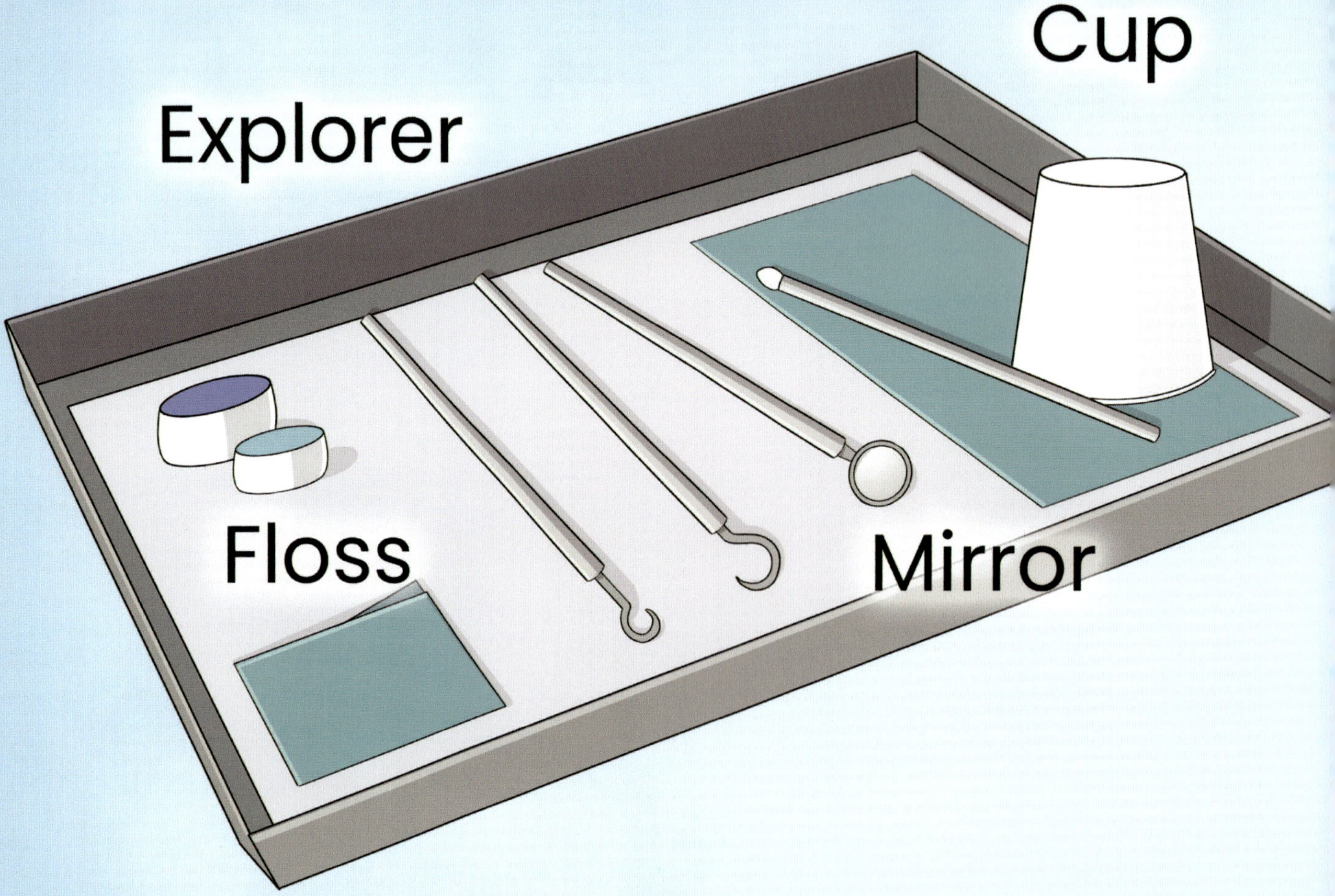

"The dental assistant will place a bib and safety glasses on you for your protection. This will allow you to be ready for X-rays, an examination, and the cleaning and polishing of your teeth," said Professor Toad.

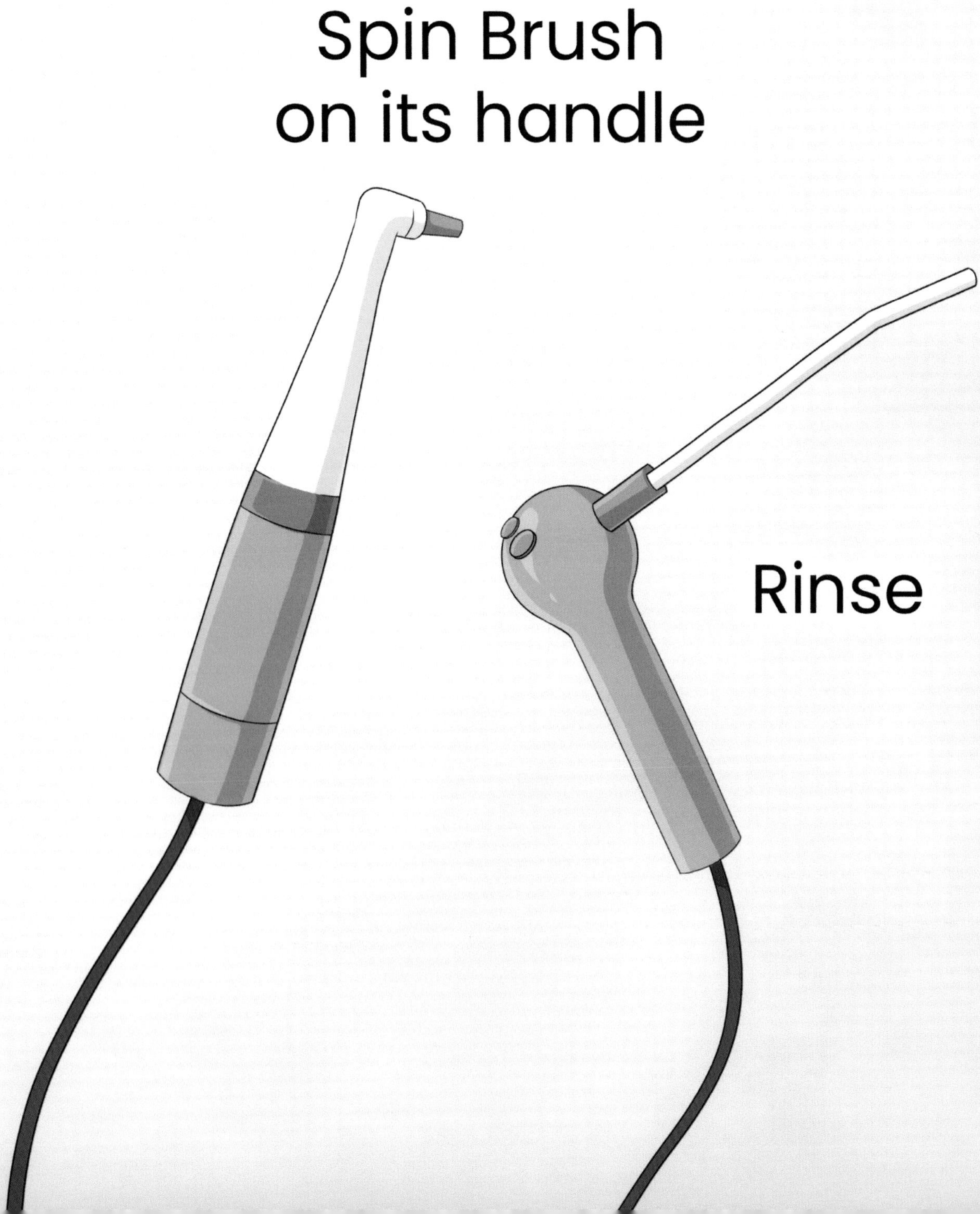
Spin Brush
on its handle
Rinse

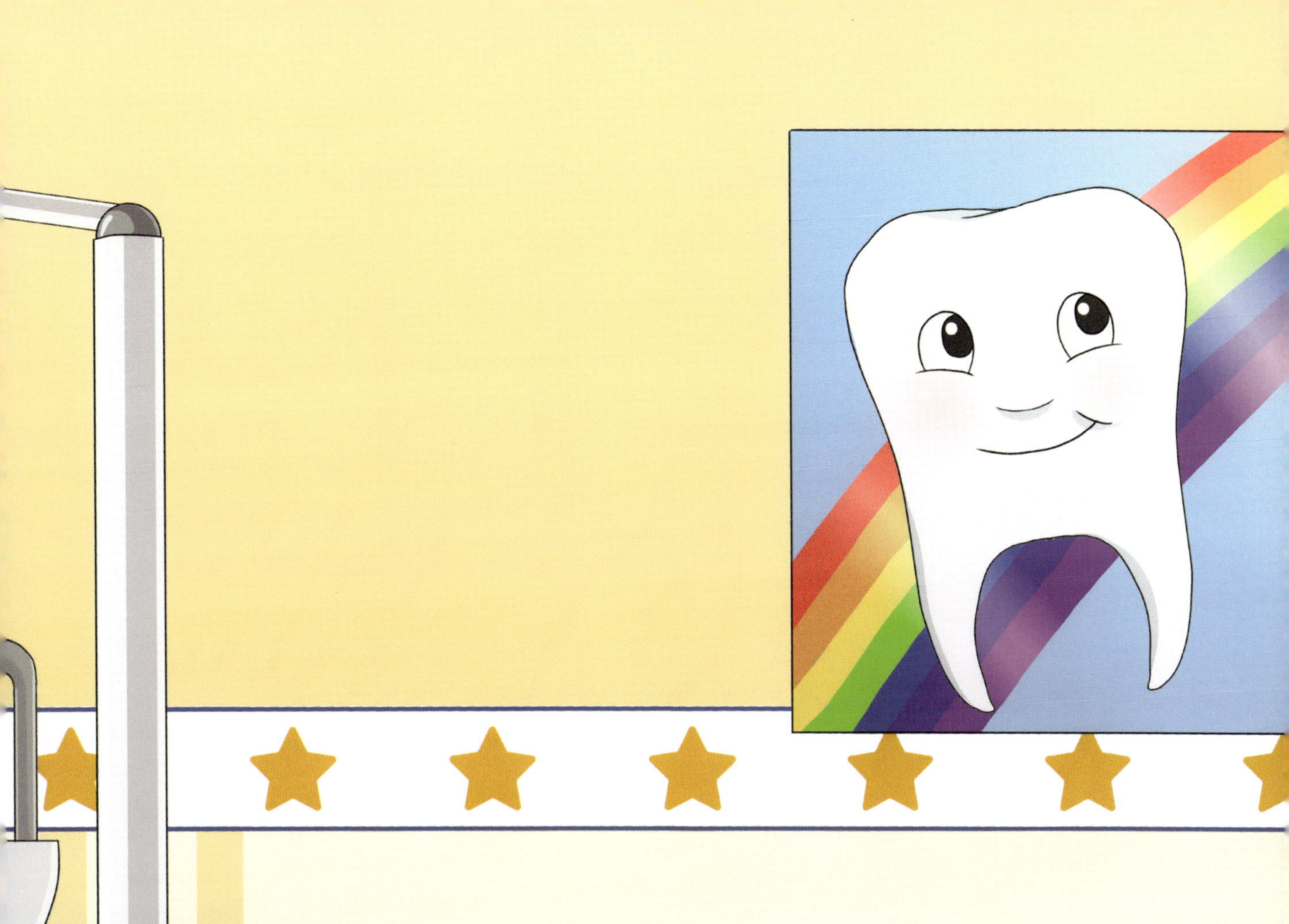

"When the dental assistant is ready to take your X-rays, she will lay a lead apron on your chest to shield you from radiation. You will be asked to open your mouth wide so the dental assistant can place the X-ray ring and film in your mouth."

"Then the X-ray head will be placed on the X-ray ring. It will take about fifteen seconds for the X-ray to be taken," explained Professor Toad.

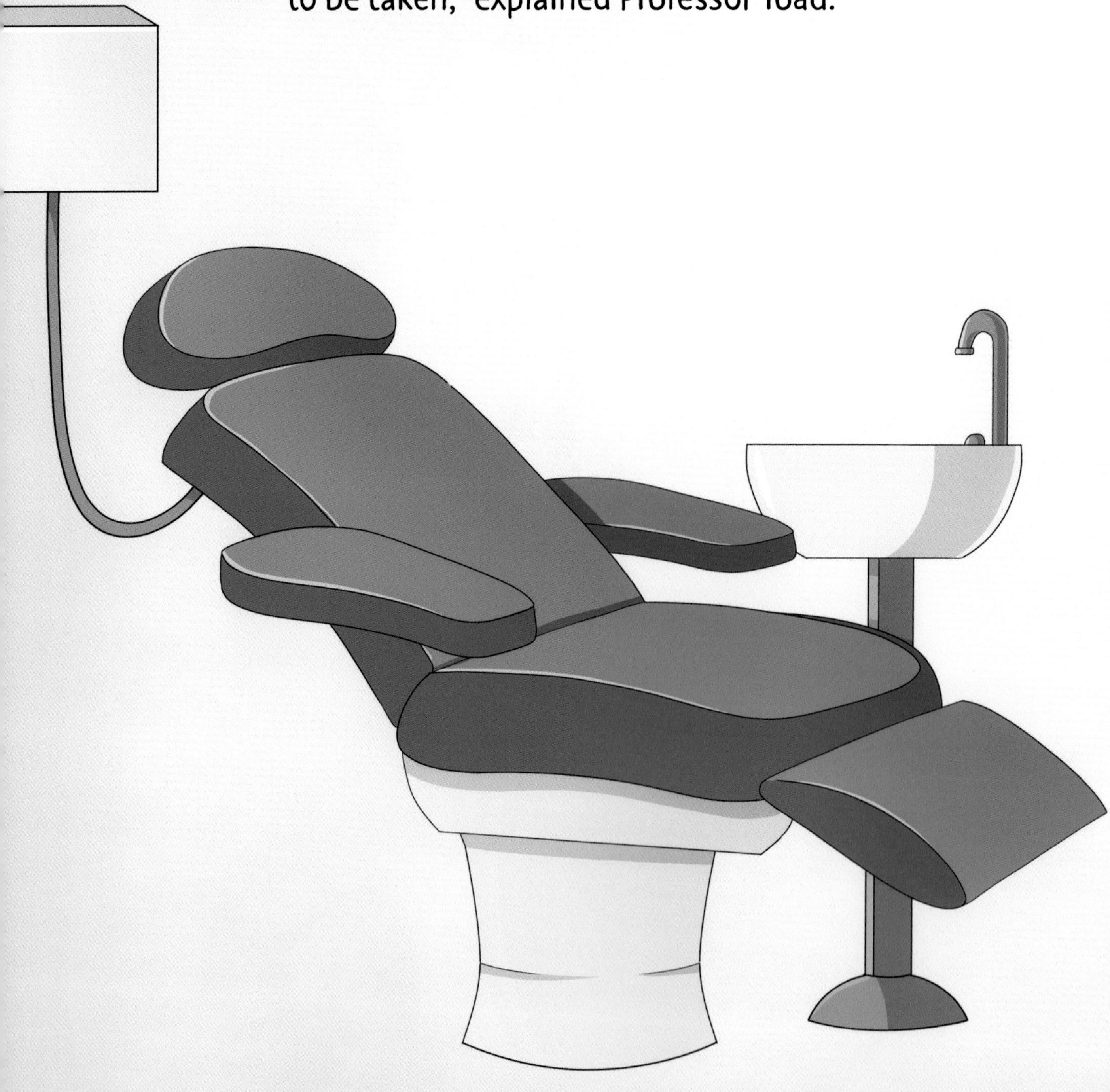

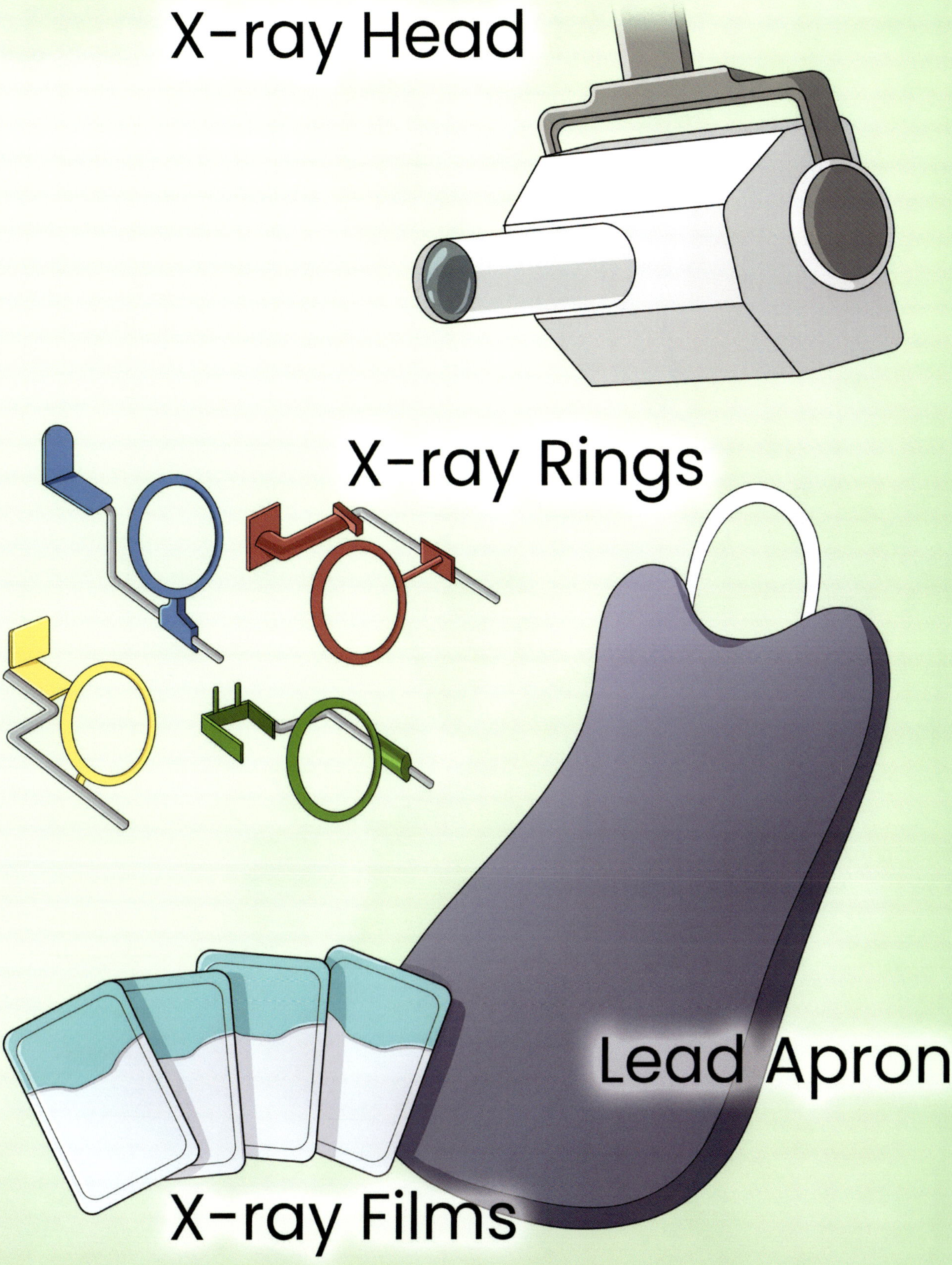
X-ray Head
X-ray Rings
Lead Apron
X-ray Films

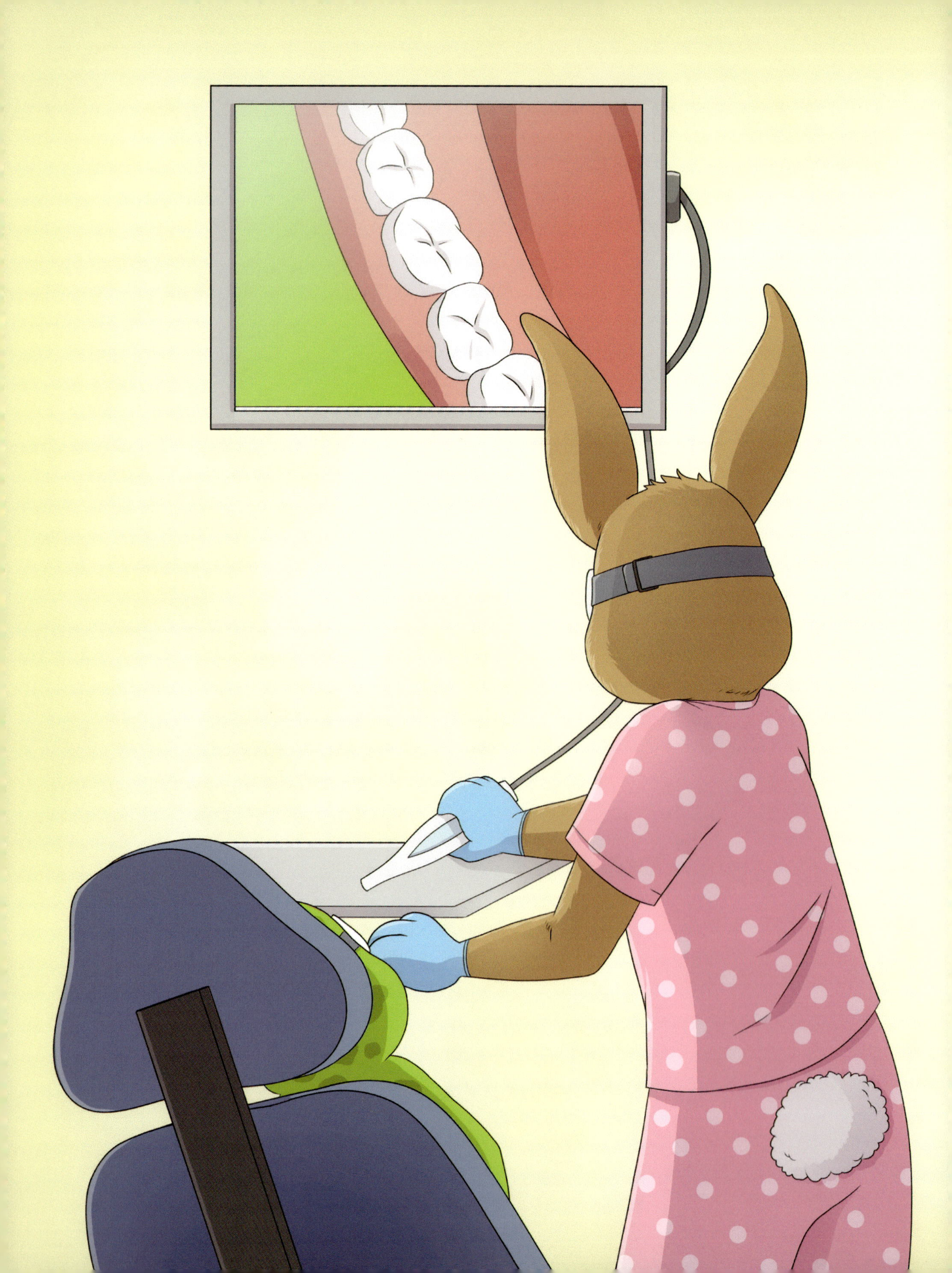

"The X-rays will show an up-close picture of your teeth," Professor Toad noted with a bright smile.

"They may also take a panoramic X-ray which requires you to stand still for about two minutes. This shows all your teeth at one time in a big view."

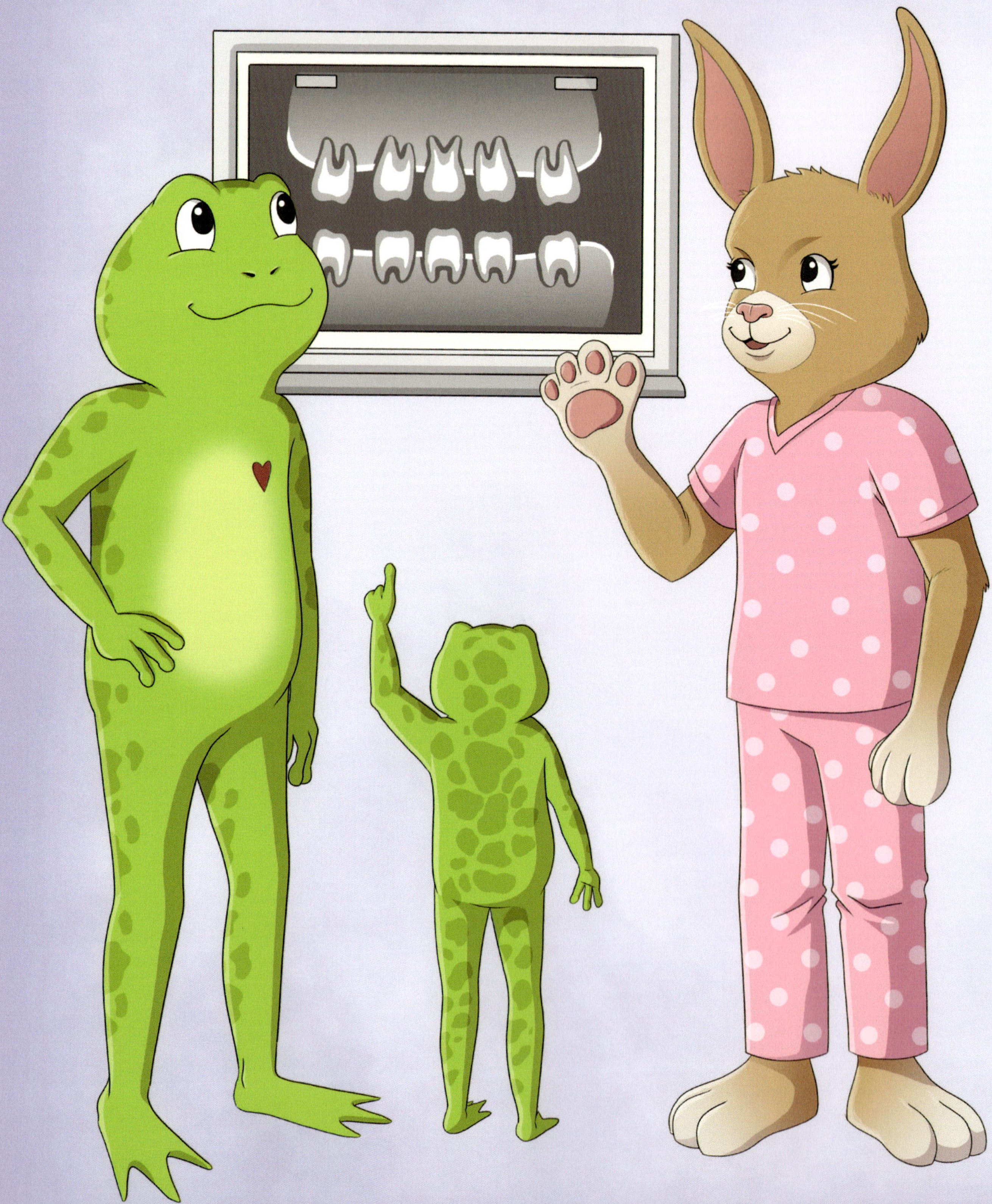

Continuing, Professor Toad said, "After the X-ray, the dental assistant will use an intra-oral camera to take a picture of any tooth that the doctor needs to examine more closely."

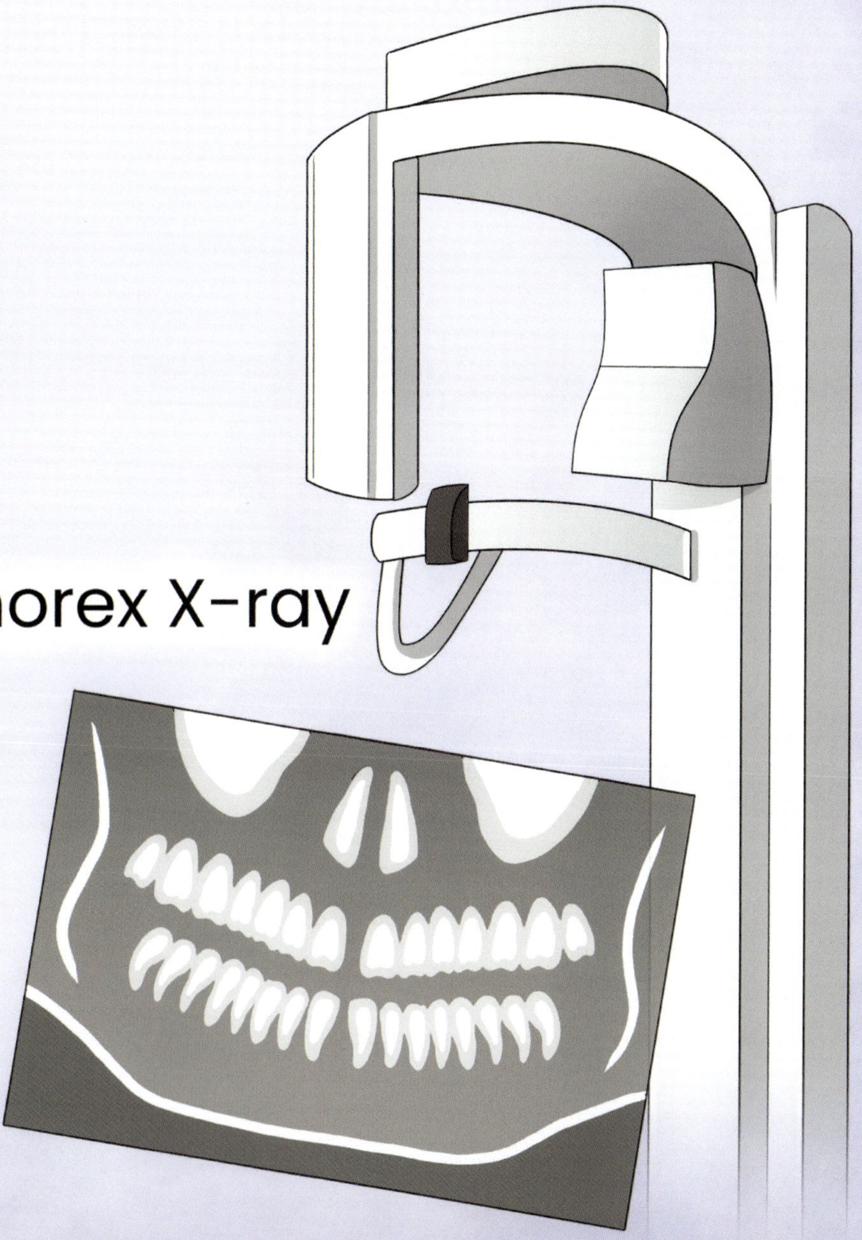

Panorex X-ray

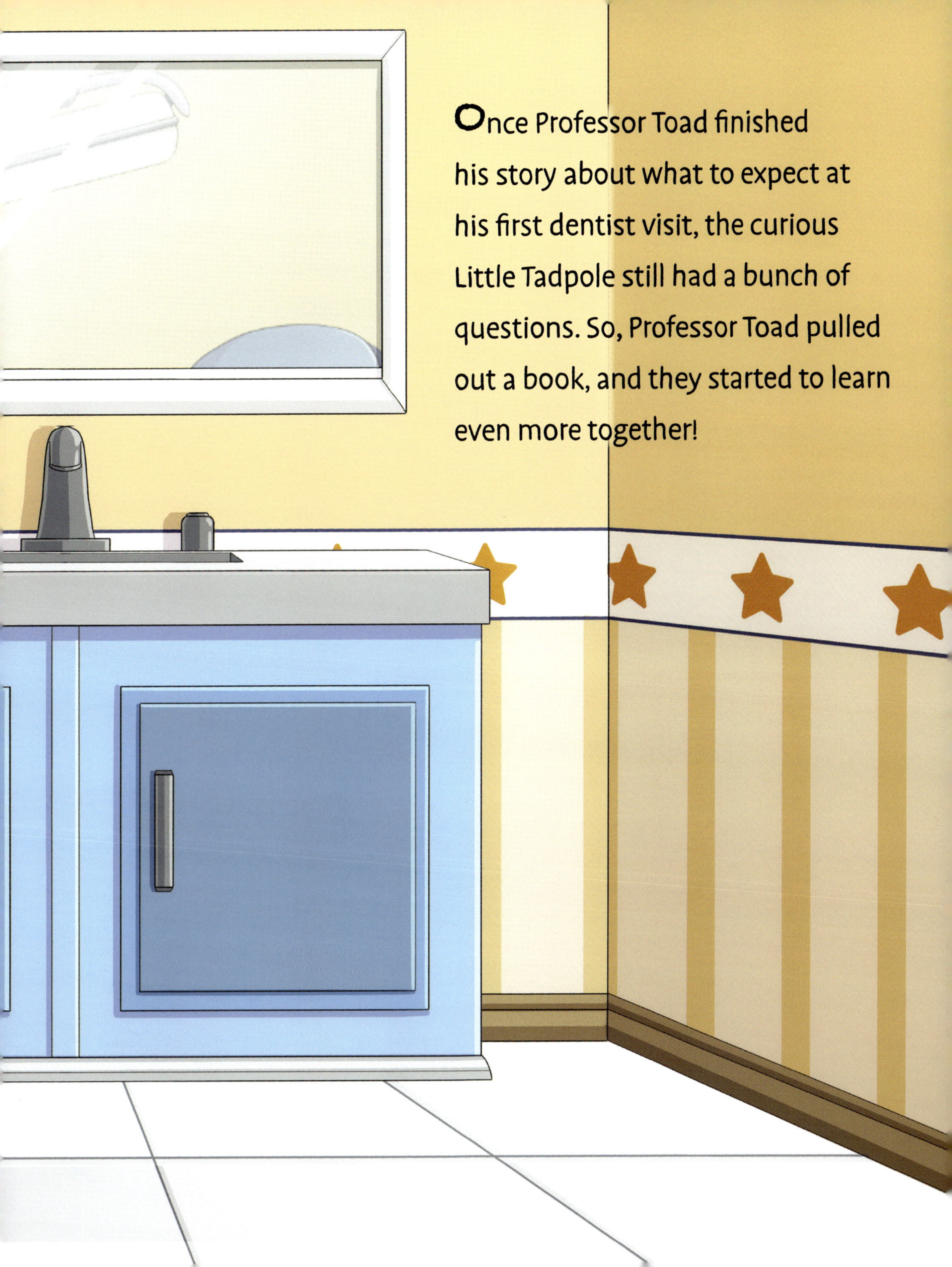

Once Professor Toad finished his story about what to expect at his first dentist visit, the curious Little Tadpole still had a bunch of questions. So, Professor Toad pulled out a book, and they started to learn even more together!

- Oral rinse will reduce your bad breath and kill bacteria up for 12 hours.
- Up to age 6 years old your teeth will be varnish, so you can eat right away.
- For ages 6 to 9 years old, you will be able to rinse your mouth. You cannot eat for 30 minutes.

A baby's teeth will shed when your permanent teeth are ready to erupt. Once your baby teeth start shedding, place them in a Tooth Fairy pillow. You must be asleep before the Tooth Fairy's magic can happen.

Tooth Fairy Pillow
Tooth Fairy Pillow

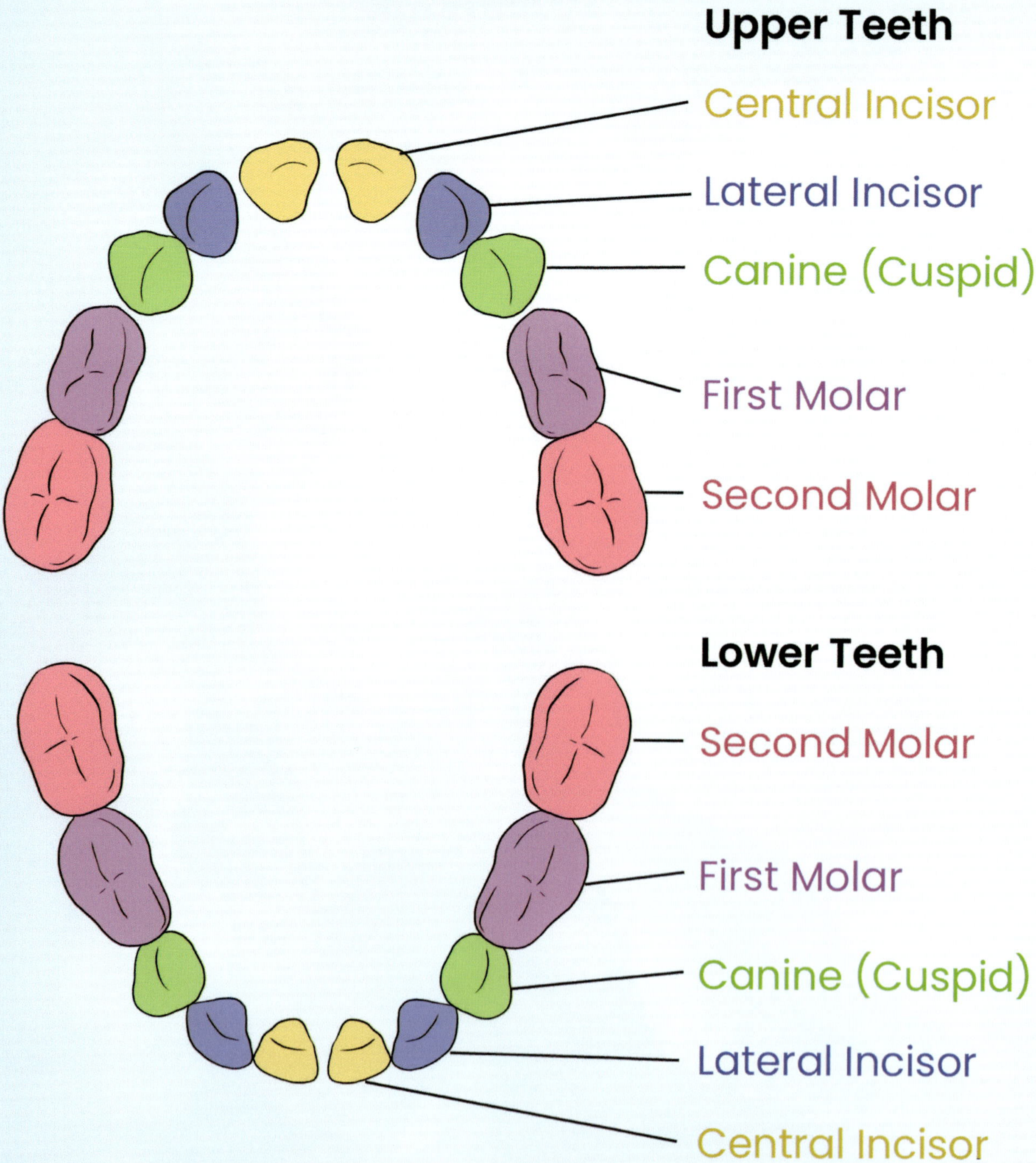
Upper Teeth
Central Incisor
Lateral Incisor
Canine (Cuspid)
First Molar
Second Molar
Lower Teeth
Second Molar
First Molar
Canine (Cuspid)
Lateral Incisor
Central Incisor

Age at Eruption (Approximate)	Shed
8-12 months	______
9-13 months	______
16-22 months	______
13-19 months	______
23-31 months	______
25-33 months	______
14-18 months	______
17-23 months	______
10-16 months	______
6-10 months	______

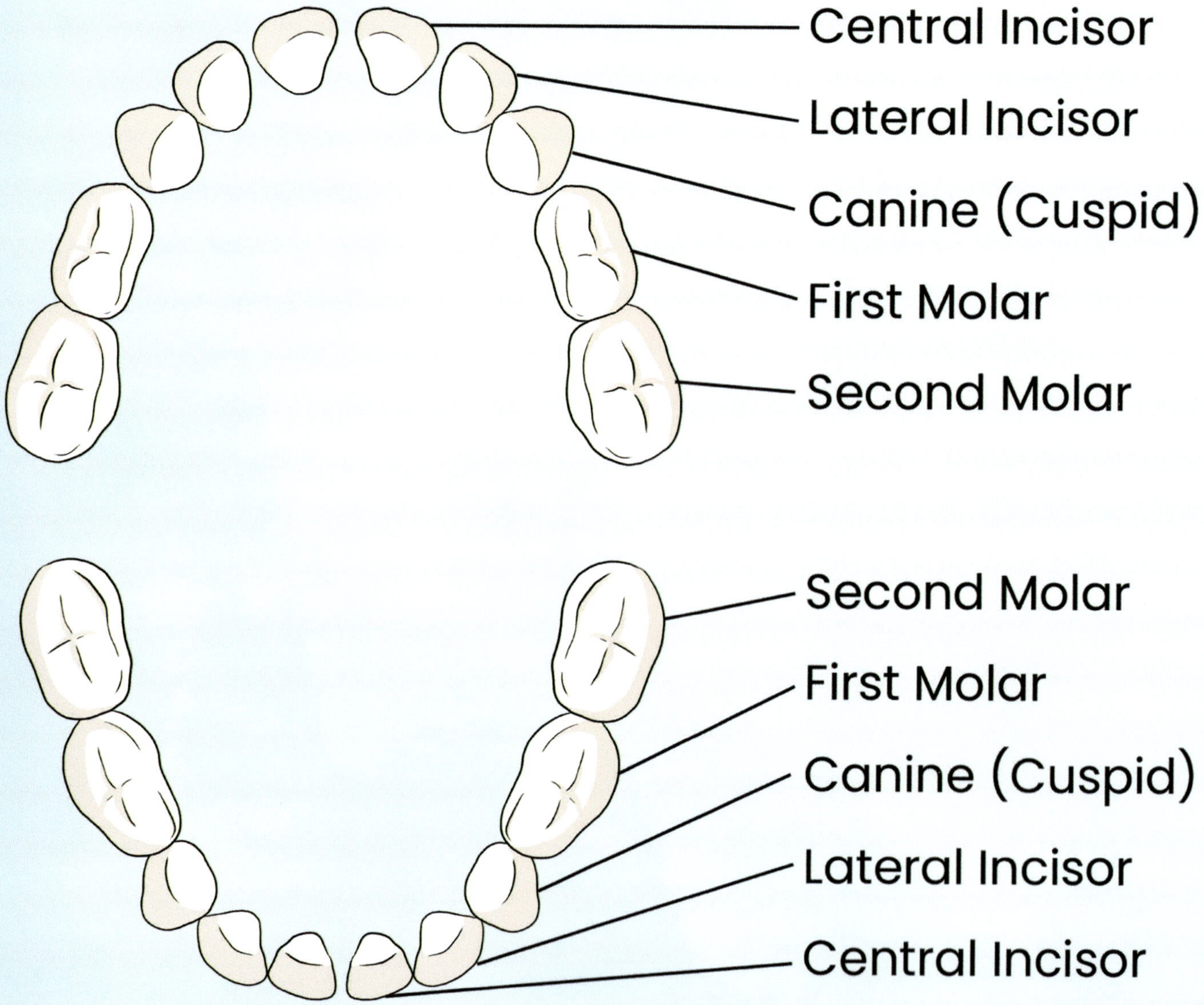
Central Incisor
Lateral Incisor
Canine (Cuspid)
First Molar
Second Molar
Second Molar
First Molar
Canine (Cuspid)
Lateral Incisor
Central Incisor

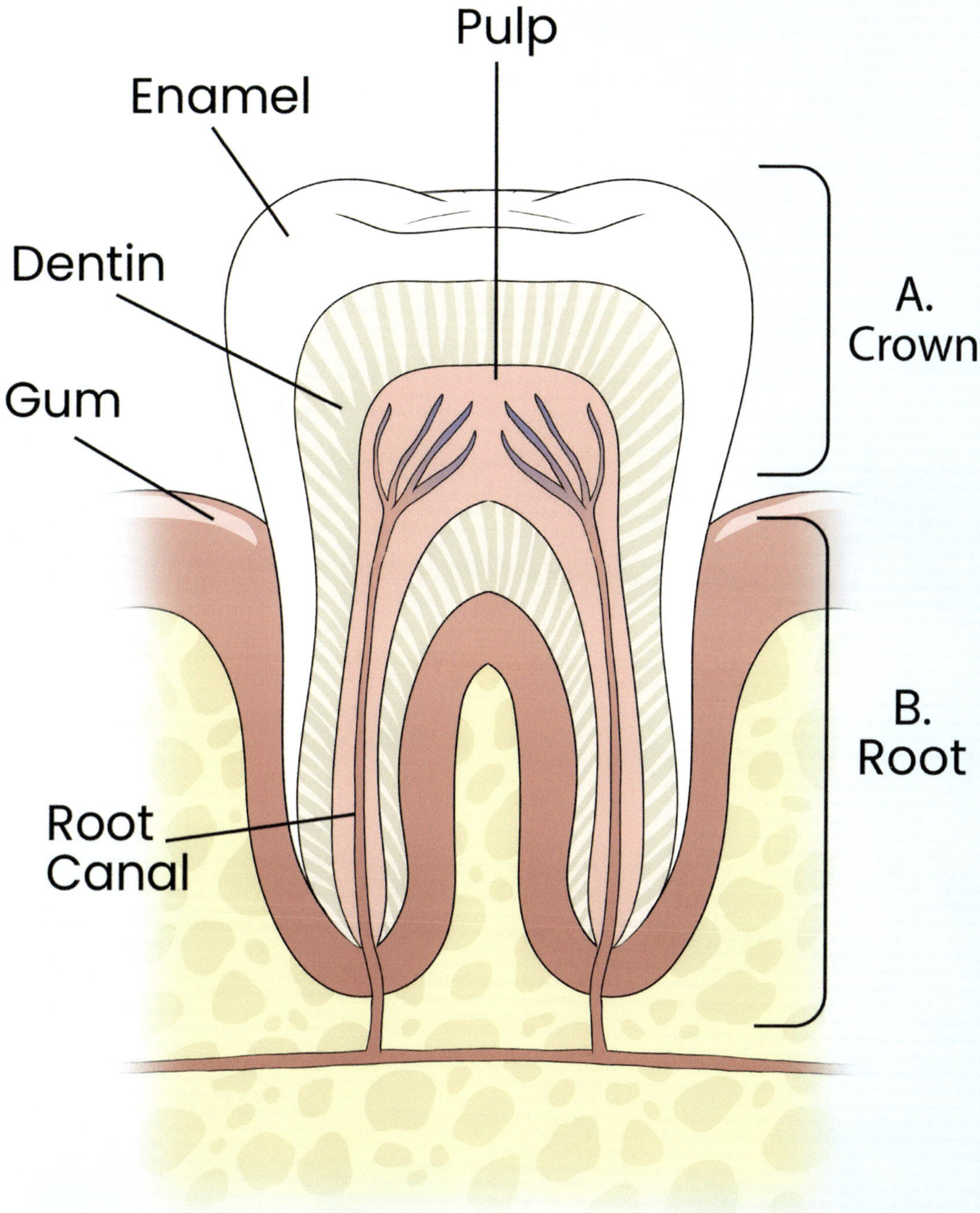
Pulp
Enamel
Dentin
Gum
Root
Canal
A.
Crown
B.
Root

About the Author

Timothy Carpenter served in the U.S. Navy for twenty-four years. He retired as an Operation Specialist Chief Petty Officer, SW/AW. He received multiple awards while serving his country, including one Navy Commendation medal, five Navy Achievement medals, and many others. Once retired, he dedicated his life to saving lives in the medical field as an Emergency Medical Technician--Intermediate. He has experienced much and decided he wanted to share some of his positive experiences through his storybooks. Tim enjoys using his creative mind to create stories to enlighten young minds and encourage questions that build confidence in the young. Timothy Carpenter resides in Fredericksburg, Virginia with his two daughters and six grandchildren.